Aa Bb Cc Dd Ee Ff

Bump in the road ahead

Traffic goes in one direction

STOP

BUMP

ONE WAY

Stop and look in all directions

Nn Oo Pp Qq Rr Ss

Watch for fallen rocks

Yield to oncoming traffic

YIELD

No trucks allowed on the road

Road is slippery when wet

Gg Hh Ii Jj Kk Ll Mm

Railroad Crossing

Do not enter this road

Traffic light ahead

Do not turn to go in the opposite direction

DO NOT
ENTER

Tt Uu Vv Ww Xx Yy Zz

Keep left of the road

KEEP
LEFT

School Crossing

Bicycles allowed on the road

Winding road ahead

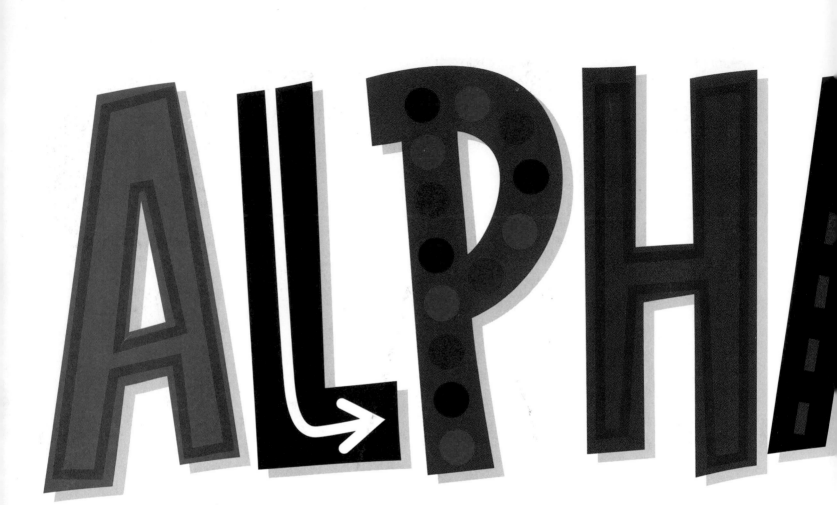

ALPHA

Beep, beep!

BEEP

A Zipping, Zooming ABC

by Debora Pearson

illustrated by Edward Miller

Holiday House / New York

Zipping, zooming down the street. . . . What's up ahead?
Come on— Beep, beep!

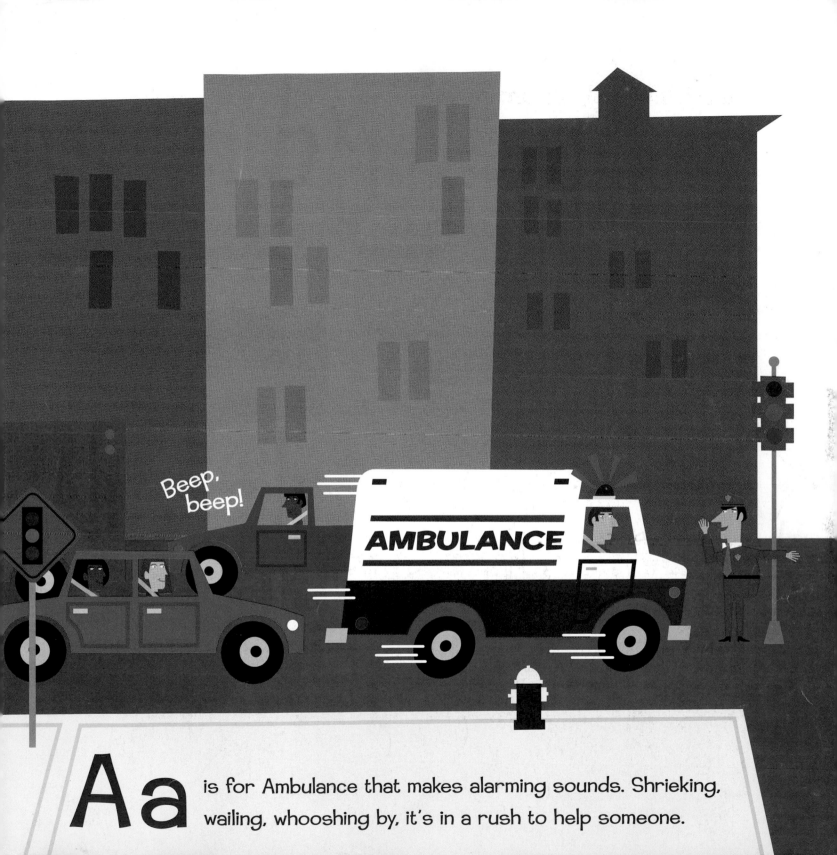

Aa is for Ambulance that makes alarming sounds. Shrieking, wailing, whooshing by, it's in a rush to help someone.

Bb

is for Bulldozer. It crawls through muck, it clears out rubble. It moves big boulders as if they are pebbles.

Cc

is for Cement Mixer. In its belly, called the drum, wet cement flip-flops around then gushes out the chute.

CITY DUMP

Dd is for Dump Truck. It thunders by with its load, stops and tips it on the ground. Clatter, crash, **ka-Boom!**

EXIT
35

Toot!
Toot!

is for Exit sign.
See you later— Toot!
Toot!

Ff is for Forklift that flits around the freight yard.
It lifts and lowers boxes with its long, steel fingers.

crunch!
grind!
crunch!
grind!

DON'T LITTER

is for Garbage Truck that growls along the road.
It's on the prowl for stinky trash to squish, crunch, gr-r-r-r-rind.

Hh

is for Hook and Ladder Truck. Hurry, hurry—race to the fire! Stretch out that ladder and douse those tall flames!

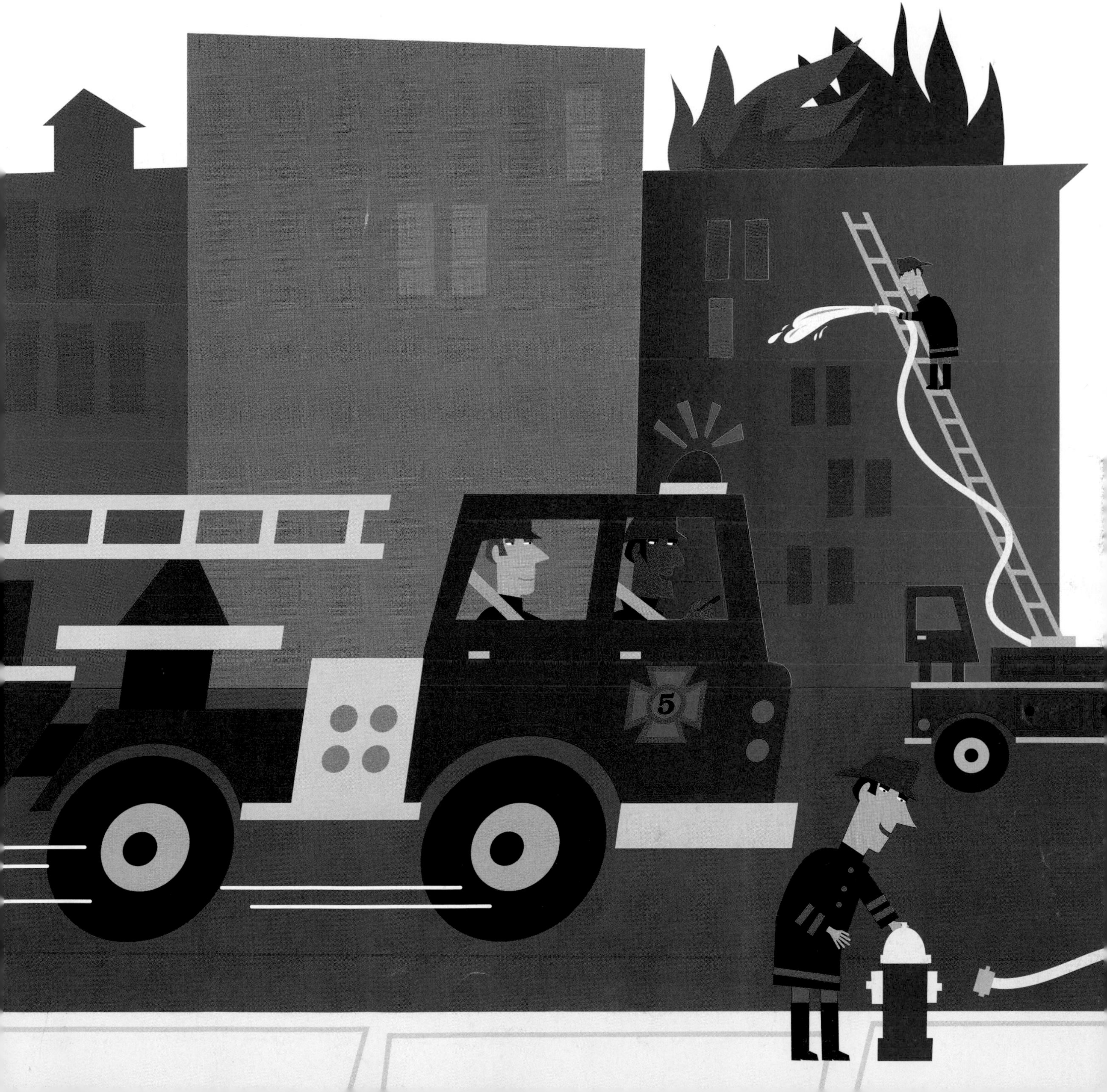
5

Ii

is for Ice-Cream Truck, a chiming, tinkling, summertime truck.
Buy a treat and lick it up—you'll feel cool instead of hot.

Jj is for Jeep. It bumps over fields, it splashes through streams. Jeeps don't need roads to get where they're going.

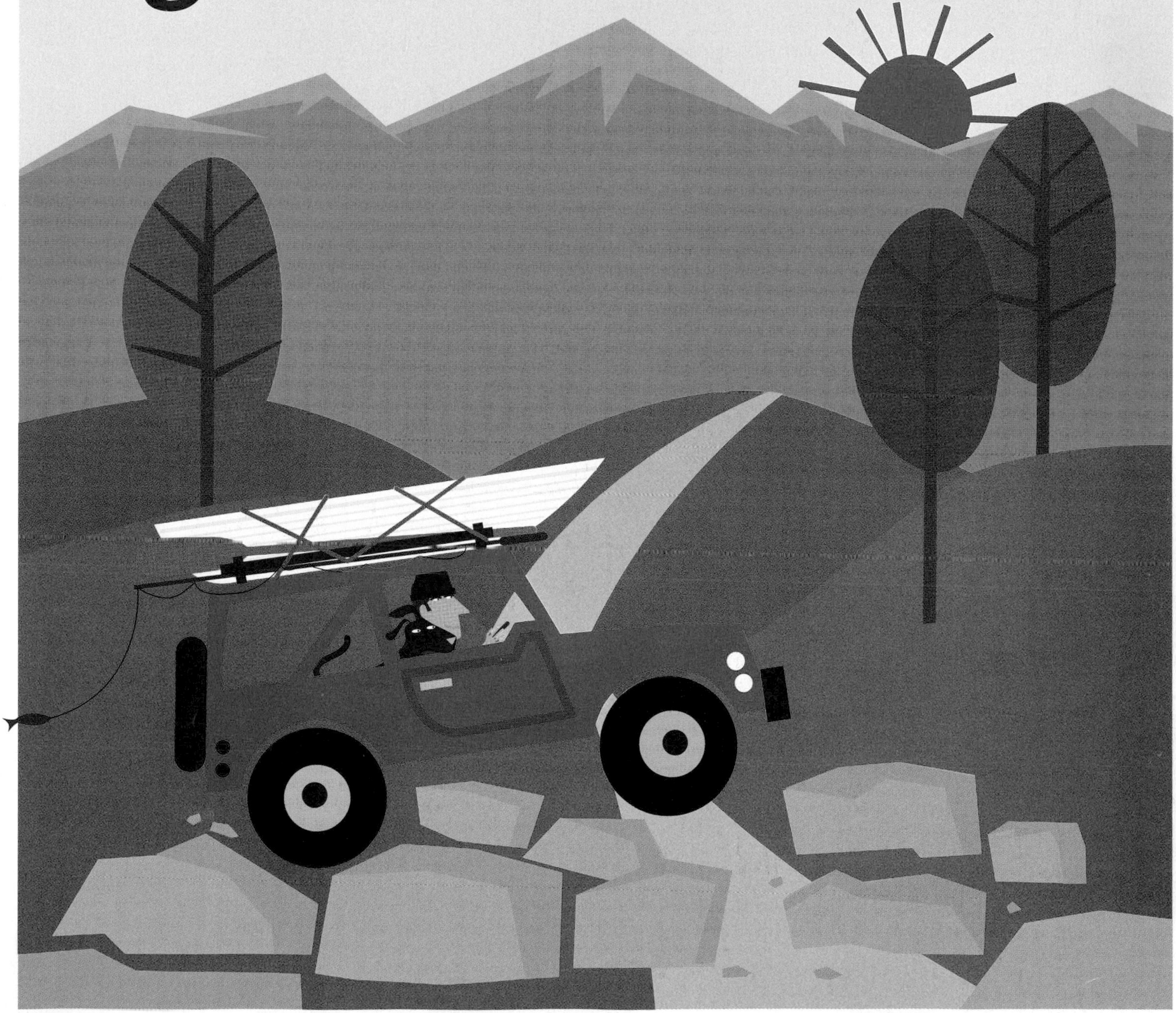

Kk

is for Keep Left sign. Follow the arrow, go where it leads or you will hear . . . Honk! Screech! Beep, BEEP!

is for Logging Truck. The tree trunks that it carries look like gigantic pencils, ready to be sharpened.

Screech!
Screech!
Screech!

BIG BART

Mm is for Moving Truck. The space is immense at the back of this truck—it can hold *EVERYTHING* found in a house.

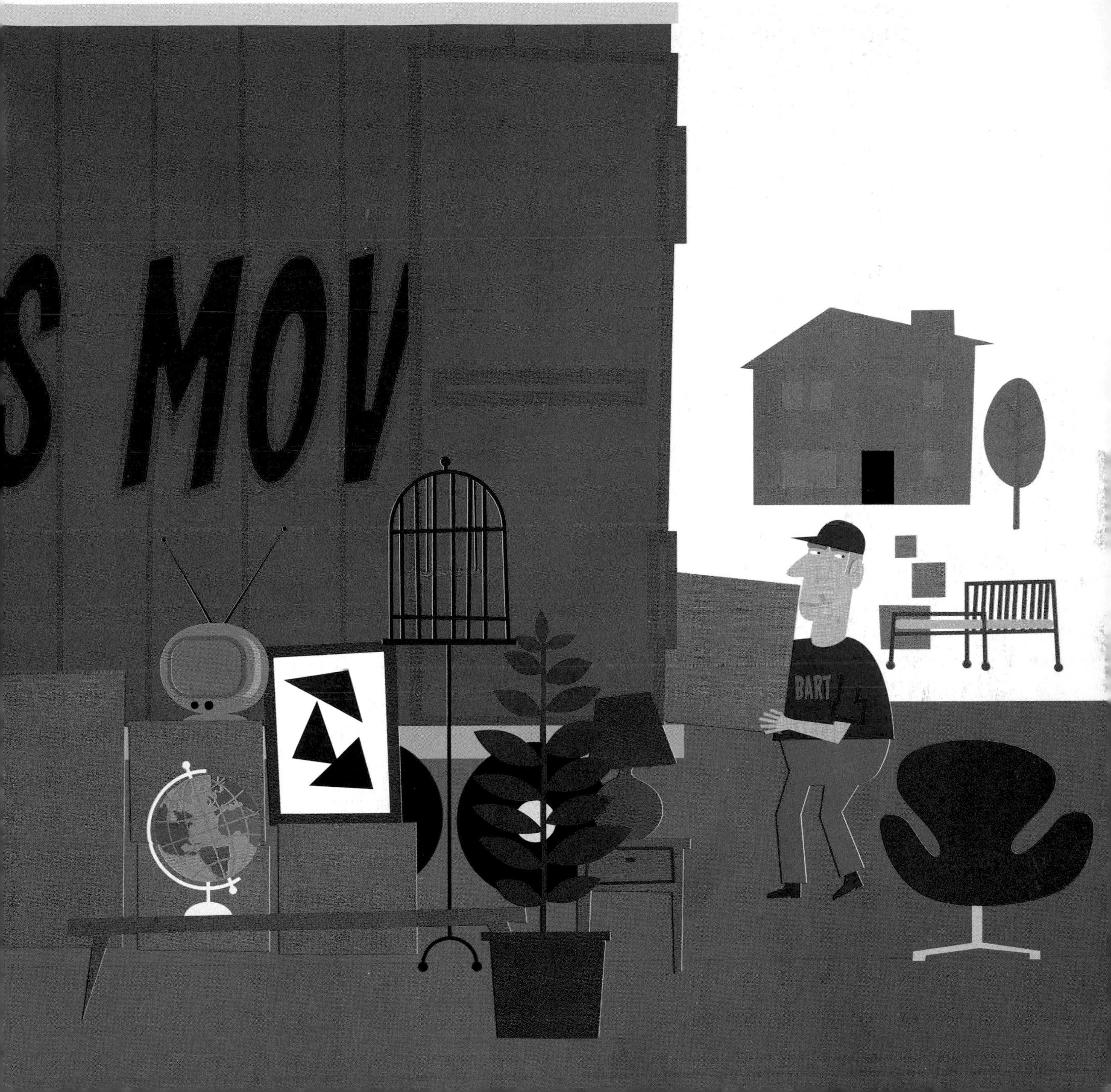
S MOV
BART

NEWSSTAND

CITY NEWS

Nn

is for Newspaper Truck, always on the move. It zooms to newsstands and delivers the papers that people read each day.

Oo

is for One Way sign. Big cars, little cars, fast and slow, all head in the same direction. Everyone goes with the flow.

Pp

is for Police Car, speeding after bank robbers. In a flash, it howls past. Its mission? Catch those thieves!

Qq

is for Quarry Excavator. It gnaws apart a tower of rubble, dropping rocks like crumbs. Its jaws can hold boulders as big as cars.

Rr is for Railroad Crossing sign. Watch out, keep back—trains roar along these tracks.

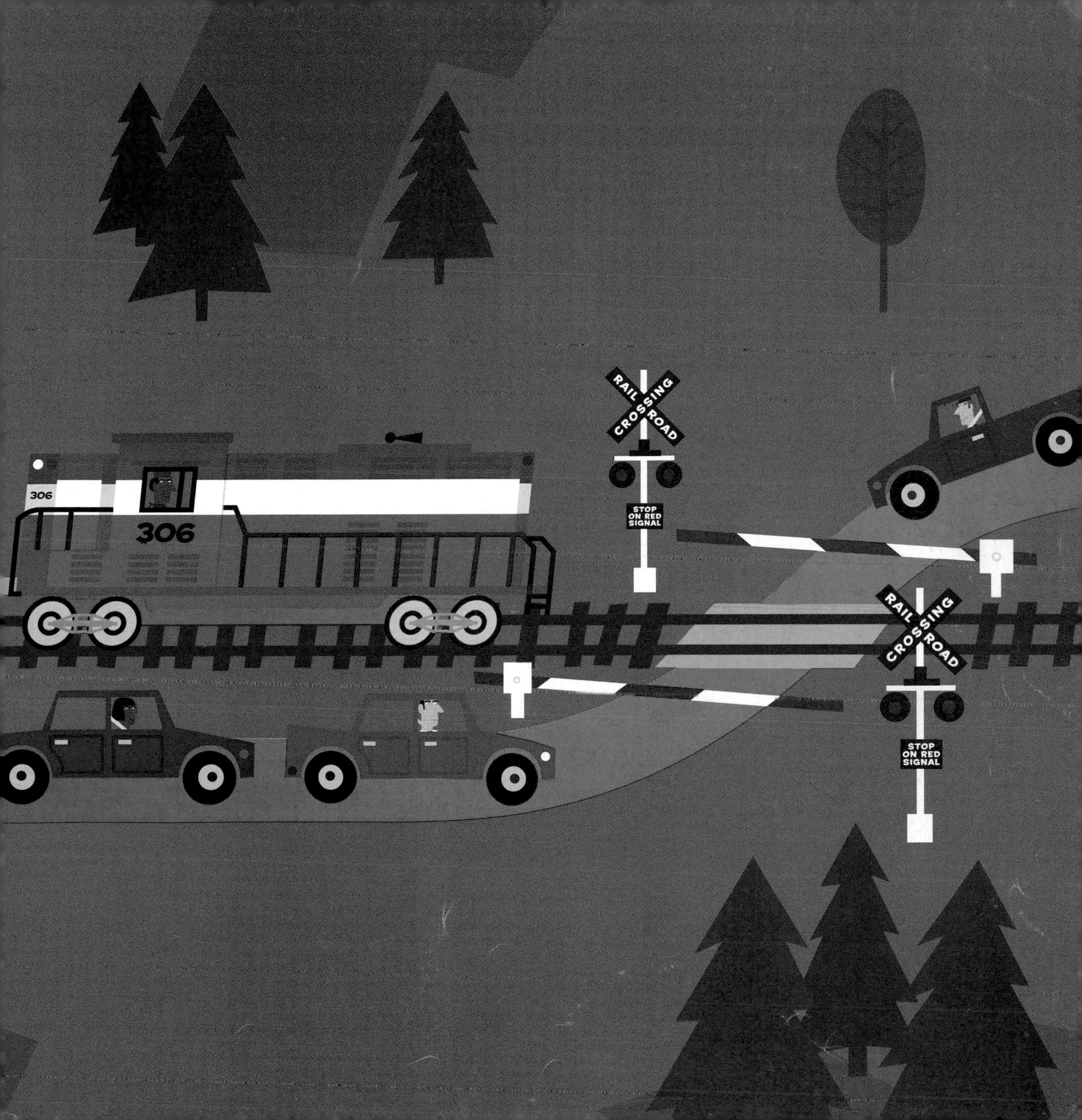
306
306
RAIL ROAD CROSSING
STOP ON RED SIGNAL
RAIL ROAD CROSSING
STOP ON RED SIGNAL

Ss

is for Street Cleaner. It scours the city in search of grime, scrubbing up dirt and devouring it.

KEEP OUR
CITY CLEAN

Tt is for Tow Truck. It goes fishing for cars with its giant hook, reeling them up and dragging them off.

Uu

is for Utility Truck that hoists a worker in its bucket. U-p . . . and u-p . . . the worker soars to fix the telephone wires.

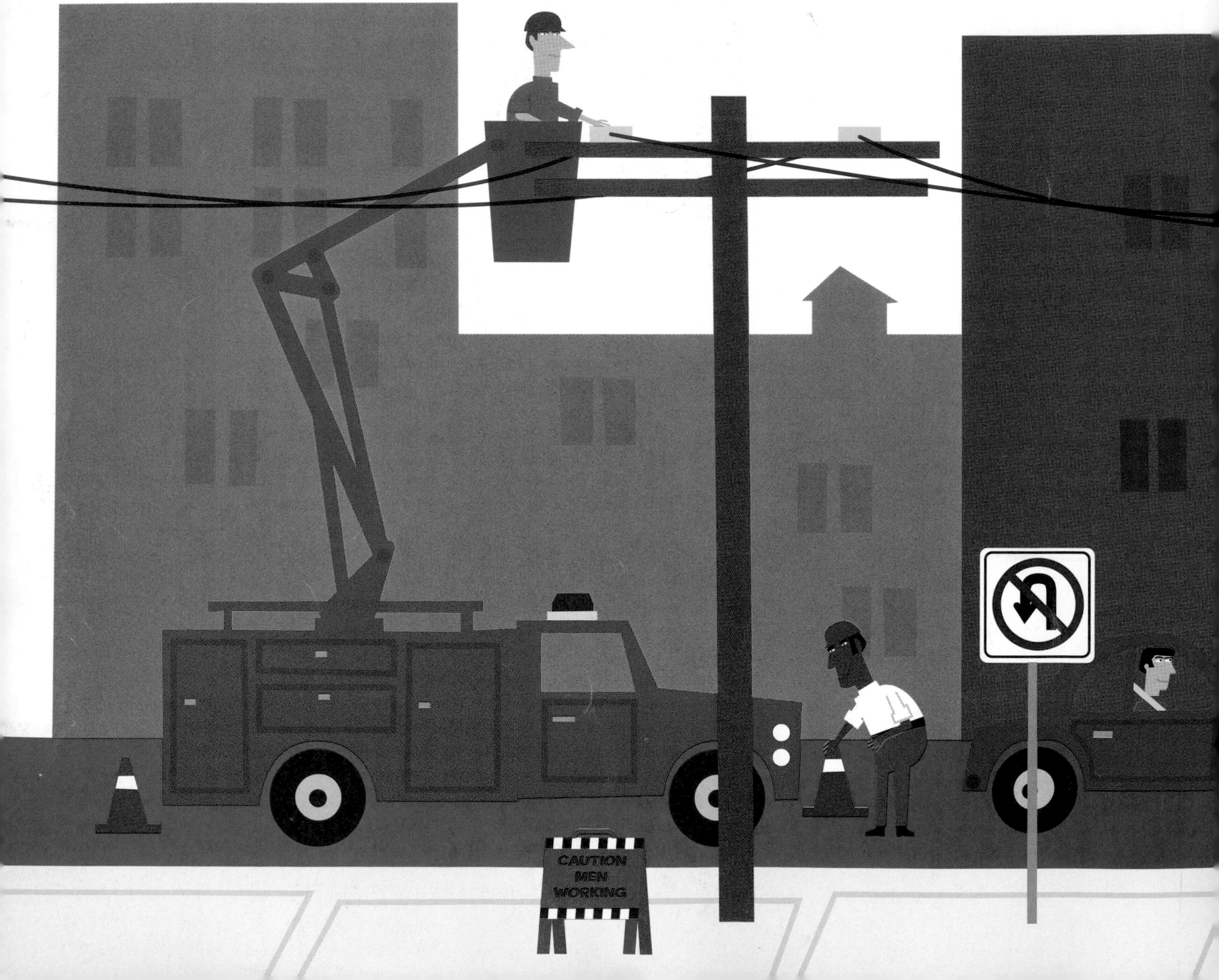
CAUTION
MEN
WORKING

V v

is for Van, darting, dashing, zigzagging through traffic.
It's busy delivering packages—
vroooooom!

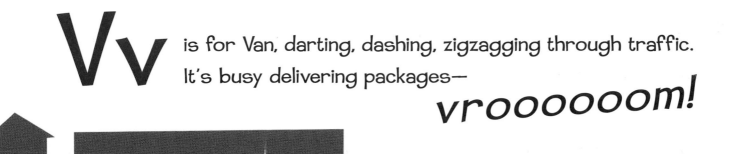

Ww is for Wrecking Crane. **WHAM!** When it swings its iron ball, buildings tumble to the ground.

CAUTION MEN WORKING

CAUTION CONSTRUCTION SITE

Xx
is for X-ray Truck that visits people who need X rays. It has a machine that takes pictures of the insides of their bodies.

FREE
X RAYS
TODAY

Yy

is for Yield sign. Take it easy, take it slow.
Make way for other cars then go, go, go.

YIELD

Zz

is for Zamboni, finishing up its work. It shaves and cleans the ice, then covers it with water. When the water freezes, it becomes new ice to skate on.

Now the busy machine creeps off to its shed. The skaters have left, the rink is closed up—it's time to go to bed.

For my son,
Benjamin, my
enthusiastic guide
to the amazing world
of cars and trucks—D. P.

For my dad, who served as a traffic
cop for the NYC Police Department
for more than 20 years—E. M.

Text copyright © 2003 by Debora Pearson
Illustrations copyright © 2003 by Edward Miller III
All Rights Reserved

Printed in the United States of America

www.holidayhouse.com

Library of Congress Cataloging-in-Publication Data
Pearson, Debora.
Alphabeep: a zipping, zooming ABC / by Debora Pearson ; illustrated by Edward Miller.—1st ed.
p. cm.
Summary: Describes a vehicle or street sign for every letter of the alphabet
from Ambulance to Zamboni.
ISBN 0-8234-1722-0
1. Motor vehicles-Juvenile literature. 2. English language—Alphabet-
Juvenile literature. [1. Vehicles. 2. Traffic signs and signals.
3. Alphabet.] I. Miller, Edward, 1964- ill. II. Title.
TL147.P43 2003
428.1 [E]-dc21
2002069053

Zamboni and the configuration of the Zamboni ice
resurfacing machine are registered by the U.S.
Patent and Trademark Office as the trademarks
of Frank J. Zamboni & Co., Inc.

Visit www.edmiller.com for fun
activities to accompany this book.

ISBN-13: 978-0-8234-1722-3 (hardcover)
ISBN-13: 978-0-8234-2076-6 (paperback)
ISBN-10: 0-8234-1722-0 (hardcover)
ISBN-10: 0-8234-2076-0 (paperback)

Aa Bb Cc Dd Ee Ff

STOP

Stop and look in all directions

Bump in the road ahead

BUMP

Traffic goes in one direction

ONE WAY

Nn Oo Pp Qq Rr Ss

Watch for fallen rocks

No trucks allowed on the road

Road is slippery when wet

Yield to oncoming traffic

YIELD

Gg Hh Ii Jj Kk Ll Mm

Railroad Crossing

Do not enter this road

Traffic light ahead

Do not turn to go in the opposite direction

DO NOT ENTER

Tt Uu Vv Ww Xx Yy Zz

Keep left of the road

Bicycles allowed on the road

KEEP LEFT

School Crossing

Winding road ahead